**For the first time since Elenda had gotten tall enough, she looked out that diamond shaped window as the elevator moved.**

She'd habitually avoided looking out at the passing floors, but Elenda was sure she would have noticed a mirror replacing the clear glass.

A pale, drawn reflection stared back at her. Elenda was horrified at the dark circles under her eyes and lines around her mouth. Her hair was even faded, as if she'd gone gray since leaving that morning. She reached toward her hair, then froze.

The woman in the mirror moved too.

She didn't touch her hair, and she certainly wasn't still and staring.

Instead, Elenda's reflection covered her face with her hands. She seemed to be crying.

Elenda backed against the wall, whispering no over and over again.

The reflection continued to sob.

**Legacy of the Land**

Published 2017 by Spiral Publishing, Ltd. www.spiralpublishing.net

Book and cover design copyright © 2017 by Spiral Publishing, Ltd.

Cover art copyright © 2017 by Littleny/Dreamstime

ISBN-13: 978-0-9908875-9-1

*To my Granny, Clinas Kilgore*

*For her love of travel,*
*her love of reading,*
*and her love of family.*

# LEGACY OF THE LAND

KARI KILGORE

# Chapter 1

THE CITY, the block, the whole neighborhood were exactly as Elenda Murphy remembered. Swarms of yellow taxis charged through crowded streets, horns honking to announce every penny added to the meter. Herds of pedestrians floated through an endless dance with the cars, interlaced flowing streams, crossing but rarely touching. Huge city buses lumbered through the chaos, moving eddies in the endless currents. The compulsive motion was so strong, so deep, that it echoed under the streets and in the skies above.

The building itself hadn't changed since before Elenda's parents were born less than a mile away. The light gray stone with red brick accents stood for years before the attack on Pearl Harbor thousands of miles away from New York City. More than half a century later, toxic debris and dust from the World Trade Center piled against the windows and seeped inside, even so far north in the Upper West Side.

Still the building endured.

Elenda's family intended to dwell here until humans were no more. She'd been the first in three generations to leave for college and never return. In more than ten years since she'd moved out and started her own life, not a thing had changed.

Nearly as constant was her mother. Marian Murphy's hair got longer and shorter, with a brief, ill-advised flirtation with permanent waves captured in photos from decades gone by. The rich, dark red color never wavered, though. Marian proudly declared that she would not go gray as long as stylists needed the work. Or in a pinch, or some sort of apocalypse, as long as she could do the job herself.

Marian's wardrobe varied as subtly as her hair did, with only shifting hemlines, heel heights, and jewelry marking the years passing. The fine, wool suiting, either black or dark gray, pantsuits or dress suits with shoes to match, were as reliable as the ball dropping in Times Square.

Elenda knew her own wardrobe of t-shirts, blue jeans, and Birkenstocks distressed her always appropriate mother. Almost as much as the curly brown hair she sometimes didn't bother cutting for months at a time. The habits she'd picked up during her teen years to play up that distress had settled into an odd style of her own. She hardly could have survived her life as an extreme adventure vacation leader with a trunk full of high heels and silk blouses.

When she was being unusually honest with herself, Elenda admitted she was as predictable as Marian. Once she recognized that flash of herself in her stubborn mother, a fragile peace and friendship grew between them. Not nearly as easygoing as her bond with her easygoing father, but satisfying all the same.

Marian parked her car, the latest in a long line of dark blue Mercedes, under the huge burgundy awning. The doorman, the only doorman Elenda could remember, darted to Mrs. Murphy's driver side door. His uniform matched the awning, down to the gleaming brass fittings.

"Mrs. Murphy," Dwight said as he opened the door. "Welcome back."

"Don't fuss over me," Marian Murphy said, flipping her hand toward Elenda. "My baby girl needs the help today."

Elenda knew her face was bright red just as well as she knew asking her mother not to call her baby girl wouldn't do any good. She did need the help. Dwight drew back and nearly ran around to her side of the car. Her arms worked just fine, but he swept the door open so fast the car rocked.

"Surgery went well, then, ma'am?"

"Very well, thank you," Elenda said. With the massive cast turning her right leg into a dead weight, she took Dwight's offered arm to pull herself out of the car. "You know I can't stand being called ma'am. I have more than enough nicknames to choose from."

"Sure thing, Len," Dwight said. His grin let Elenda know he enjoyed the exchange as much as she did. "How long you here for?"

"She's here just as long as she needs to be," Elenda's mother said. "She's welcome to stay forever and a day if she wants." She stood behind Dwight, beckoning to the junior doorman. "Please bring my daughter's things up."

The young man hovering behind Dwight's shoulder was the first new thing Elenda had noticed since they'd left the hospital. Dwight pulled her crutches out of the back seat. Refusing to accept a wheelchair was one battle Elenda managed to win in this whole procedure. She settled the handles into her already bruised armpits and made her slow, hesitant way toward the revolving glass doors.

"This thing will be on for at least six weeks," Elenda said, finally answering part of Dwight's question. She wasn't ready to think about the *at least* part of that sentence. "Just depends on how long it takes my kneecap to heal."

"Then you have your physical therapy," Marian said,

nodding once. "Use the side door, sweetheart. That will be so much easier."

Dwight was already halfway to the main doors to lock them open, something he routinely did for deliveries. He glanced at Elenda. She half-smiled and nodded. She couldn't afford to get into battles before they even made it inside. Not when her first real challenge, and the one she'd been dreading since these arrangements were made weeks ago, waited in the lobby.

## Chapter 2

THE ELEGANT BRASS continued throughout the echoing, dark green marble floored room. The mellow gleam lined the front desk, mailboxes, and even the seams between the massive slabs of rock. The attention to detail reflected the taste and healthy budget of the building's designers, Elenda's distant ancestors.

The most elaborate, and most expensive, display was the antique elevator. A mere twenty-two steps had carried Elenda past the terrifying thing and into the staircase at the back of the lobby ever since she'd been old enough to throw a big enough tantrum to make it happen.

The elaborate bars and spirals of the elevator's double doors had long ago been covered with glass. Despite everyone telling her it was to protect the original fittings, Elenda was certain one too many little girl's fingers had fallen victim to the ancient elevator.

Her own had in countless nightmares as far back as she could remember. Her mother's tales of how much freedom and lack of supervision she'd had growing up in the 1970s only confirmed that certainty.

An arc of brass numbers and a matching arrow above the door warned of the impending arrival. Perhaps worst of all, at least on this floor and before she stepped into the claustrophobic box, was the key. Again under glass like some kind of sinister crown jewel, a long brass skeleton key hung beside a keyhole.

The fire fighter's access explanation rang hollow to Elenda at age eight and still at twenty-eight. The elevator car was shaped like nothing more than a metal cage. A fearful, and powerful, part of her mind insisted that key would never be enough to get the victim out of that cage once it slammed closed.

"Suppose you won't be taking the stairs on this visit," Dwight said, echoing her thoughts.

Elenda knew she'd never make it up eight flights even without the snail's pace as she tried to work out how to navigate on the slick floor on crutches. She'd either pass out from the pain of the cast dragging on her hip, or she'd miss a step and add a broken neck to her surgically rebuilt kneecap.

Still, she considered.

"She'll be just fine on this perfectly safe elevator," Marian said. Her flawlessly outlined red lips compressed before she smiled. "Your father made a point of checking on the most recent inspection, Elenda. Three weeks ago."

"That's wonderful timing," Elenda said. She flinched when the bell rang. Hopefully no one saw it. "Right around the time I had my little adventure on a perfectly safe staircase."

The doors were still for a second, long enough for hope to flare in Elenda's chest. Maybe the damned thing was broken. The left door slid behind the right one then, quickly enough for her to notice the burgundy carpeted floor of the car settling to almost level with the white marble threshold.

"A staircase?" Dwight said. He stepped in behind the

young man with her bags and her mother, holding one hand in front of the door to keep it from closing.

Elenda gripped the crutches with sweaty palms, wondering if her pounding heart would be enough to send her crashing to the floor. The thought of being half in, half out, with those doors poised to take out her middle, got her moving.

"I was avoiding another creaky old thing like this one," she said, letting go of one crutch so she could hold the cool polished rail. "On a ski trip in Colorado. I did great on the slopes, but fell down the main staircase on a tour of the hotel."

"A ghost tour," Marian said, amusement plain in her voice. "Her girlfriends say one of the spirits pushed her."

"It was spirits all right," Elenda said. "One too many pumpkin whiskeys down at the bar."

The door slid closed, sealing Elenda inside with her mother and the two men.

She wanted to close her eyes as well, but that felt like courting trouble. The bars and spirals on the walls were also covered with glass, and glowing white plastic buttons took the place of hand operation. The handle was still there, though, perpetually locked into the neutral straight up position. The brass panel with raised instructions about emergency operation were somehow not the least bit reassuring.

"The same thing since she left for college," Marian said. She glanced at Dwight with on eyebrow raised. "My baby girl does all these absurdly risky things outdoors. Whitewater rafting, skydiving, mountain climbing. Never even a scratch. But get her indoors and all hell breaks loose."

"Bones too," Elenda said with a tight smile.

Her stomach rolled when they lurched into motion. She stared at the letters on the emergency panel, the paisley-patterned carpet, the glass and brass fixture in the ceiling.

7

Anything to avoid looking at the diamond-shaped window in the door. Elenda had no desire to see what was floating past, or what waited on each of the floors as hidden steel cables lifted them upward.

"Well, you just let me know if there's anything I can do for you," Dwight said. His thick gray eyebrows were drawn down along with the corners of his mouth. Elenda knew he'd noticed how badly she was sweating.

"What she needs most is rest," her mother said. "And staying off her feet. Easier said than done with this one, ever since she took her first steps."

The door started to open before they stopped moving. Elenda's hand slipped on the rail, hot and slick now instead of clean and chilly. She hoped whoever got in here next wouldn't touch it.

When the floors were finally level, everyone stepped out, with Dwight once again holding his hand in front of the door. Marian Murphy turned right and disappeared, bustling down the hall. Elenda walked as steadily as she could out of the box of death.

When her foot and both crutches were on the solid, unmoving dark brown carpet, she remembered to breathe again. Elenda didn't care whether Dwight understood the reasons for her lightheadedness. She was grateful for his hand on her shoulder.

"I'll be fine from here, Dwight," she said, dropping all formalities now that her mother was out of sight. "I doubt I'll be leaving this apartment before it's time to get the cast off."

"Then I'll be praying for you, Elenda." He grinned as he walked with her down the hall, keeping pace with her hobbling progress. "On a more useful note, seriously, don't hesitate to let me know if you need anything at all. If I can't take care of it myself, I'll find someone who can."

## Chapter 3

ELENDA WAITED in the hall with her eyes closed, breathing deeply, willing everyone else to stay in their apartments. There were only three others on this floor, so if the proverbial luck of the Irish were with her indoors for a change, she'd be fine. Two of the three units being occupied by her own elderly relatives and her careful scheduling during her parents' workdays increased her odds considerably.

Six weeks to the day had passed since she'd ridden the elevator up here, just as she'd expected. She'd managed to survive forty-two long days and nights of intense interest and attention from not only her parents, but from each and every one of her family members living in the building and across the city. Several added to the fun by making the trip from out of town for her twenty-ninth birthday a couple of weeks ago.

A huge stack of library books, on-demand movies, and video chats with her friends got her through. A bit of the whiskey that helped lead to this, shipped by those friends from Colorado for her birthday, filled in the gaps once she didn't need the pain pills anymore.

She heard the whoosh before the chime, and felt the brush of air from gaps around the door. Only one door up here, but still that same brass under glass. Another key, out in the open unlike the one downstairs, gave the residents of the family penthouse floor the option to turn the elevator to express or access the basement and subbasement. A leftover from her great-great-great-great-grandfather's reign as builder-owner that struck Elenda as incredibly selfish with only one elevator in the building. That and she wasn't sure why anyone would want to get down below the foundation if they weren't forced to.

She stepped forward, steady with the crutches despite her unease with where she was. Weeks of practice and her insistence on moving under her own power made all the difference. Her stomach dropped when the elevator did.

Elenda met the waiting hospital shuttle van, more determined than ever to return without her massive plaster anchor. She knew physical therapy and building her strength back up awaited, but anything had to be better than the endless weeks she'd just been through. After more unlucky injuries than she cared to admit, she had the recovery steps down to a science. This would be a literal walk in the park.

She'd never been more mistaken in her life.

# Chapter 4

WHEN DWIGHT OPENED the van door four hours later, Elenda didn't bother trying to hide her ordeal. She could have taken a shower or even changed out of her sweaty clothes at the hospital. Her mother's expert training and top of the line cosmetics likely would have hidden how pale Elenda was. None of those things mattered more than getting upstairs and off her sobbing legs.

"You okay, Elenda?"

"I've been better, Dwight. Has the pharmacy delivery made it?"

"Upstairs already. First physical therapy?"

Far from being proud and stubborn, she nodded, took both his hands, and let him pull most of her weight up. Her back joined in the chorus of agony. The shuttle driver met them with both sets of her crutches, the original full-length ones and a shorter set.

Now that she was only wearing a leg brace and well on her way to recovery, shorter crutches would be enough. So said the cruelest physical therapist to ever walk the earth on perfectly healthy legs.

"Let me help you upstairs," Dwight said, waving another car forward.

"I'd rather you didn't. I have to get used to it. Besides, I stink like a goat at the moment. If someone could bring those short crutches up later, that would be a huge help."

He frowned, but one of the more demanding residents was already headed his way. Elenda put on her best fake smile and moved slowly through the side door.

Her fantasies of a smooth and easy recovery, made possible by years of climbing so many stairs, dissolved when the cast came off. Those huge and strong leg muscles had wasted far more than she'd expected, especially in her pale, scrawny right leg. She'd managed not to cry at the sight, but only barely. She'd cried openly through the stretching exercises that followed.

Elenda made it to the elevator without anyone speaking to her, and she barely glanced up as the doors opened on an empty car. She was so grateful and exhausted that she stepped inside and pushed the button for the top floor without wondering who'd called it.

For the first time since she'd gotten tall enough, she didn't avoid looking out that diamond shaped window as the car moved. Elenda wasn't focusing on anything besides the blessed opiates waiting in her parents' apartment.

She'd habitually avoided looking out at the passing floors, but Elenda was sure she would have noticed a mirror replacing the clear glass.

A pale, drawn reflection stared back at her. Elenda was horrified at the dark circles under her eyes and lines around her mouth. Her hair was even faded, as if she'd gone gray since leaving that morning. She reached toward her hair, then froze.

The woman in the mirror moved too.

She didn't touch her hair, and she certainly wasn't still and staring.

Instead, Elenda's reflection covered her face with her hands. She seemed to be crying.

Elenda backed against the wall, whispering no over and over again.

The reflection continued to sob.

The bar pressed sharply against her aching lower back. Her heart pounded, and fresh sweat covered her body. One of her crutches crashed to the floor.

The woman in the reflection jerked her hands away at the noise, staring intently into Elenda's eyes.

Before she managed to force enough air into her paralyzed lungs to scream, the door opened. She bolted out, not caring what floor she was on, kicking the crutch as she went.

Elenda would crawl up the stairs if she had to.

She hit the wall hard enough to knock her multi-great grandfather's portrait off the wall. The heavy oval wooden frame hit the carpet, but the curved glass didn't break. Liam O'Dowd still gazed out into a world a hundred years past his own death. Black hair parted down the middle, pale middle-aged face emotionless, as if determined to reject countless changes in and around the building he'd brought to life by the considerable force of his will.

"That did not happen," Elenda said in a flat voice.

The elevator door stood open for what seemed like an eternity before it finally closed. As it dropped, she saw her own blue eyes in that tiny window. Red-rimmed, tear-streaked, and staring.

# Chapter 5

THE LAST THING Elenda wanted was to make the long, painful journey down the quiet hall to her parents' empty apartment. Her original plan of taking two of her new pills so she could escape from pain into sleep felt like the worst idea she'd ever had.

One of the many reasons she'd hated that elevator so, and refused to ride in it from the time she was nine, was the horrible nightmares. She never knew if she'd be dropped hundreds of feet, shot miles into the air, caught in a vast space with dozens of oblivious passengers, or squeezed by shrinking walls until her racing heart woke her.

She'd felt the car jerked sideways or backward, the brass under glass walls replaced with billowing loose fabric, barely enough to keep her inside. Sometimes not enough to keep her inside.

Constantly when she was little, and even as an adult when Elenda was too tired or stressed out, the moving brass cage in her family's building turned her sleep into torture.

Whether her own changed face in the window was a

pain-induced hallucination or not, she couldn't stand those same nightmares intruding on her waking life.

Elenda turned left instead of right, picking up her crutch but leaving the portrait where it was. She'd have to deal with that later. Her hands were shaking too badly to do anything but knock the glass against the wall and shatter the whole thing. She hobbled to the end of the hall and knocked on the heavy six-panel door before she could reconsider.

Before Elenda counted to ten, a small, white-haired woman opened the door.

"Oh Lendy dear! Such a wonderful surprise! Come inside, get off of your poor knee."

Elenda sighed when the door closed between her and the elevator. The layout of the apartment was as large and sprawling as the others on the top floor, with arched door-ways, herringbone wood floors, and ten-foot ceilings accented with dramatic, hand-painted crown molding. Her grandmother's dark wooden furniture, much of it older than her seventy-two years, completed the feeling of stepping back in time.

"Come into the kitchen, you look a fright," the older woman said. "Have you brought that book I asked you about?"

"Oh, I'm sorry, Gram. I just got back from the doctor. I didn't have a chance to go down there."

Her grandmother smiled and waved her hands, then turned to start the teakettle.

"Good news from the doctor, I hope?"

"Great news. Everything's healing faster than they expected. Gonna take me a long while to build my leg back up, though."

"Well, you'll be safe and comfortable here," her grand-mother said. She set out two dark green china cups and saucers, then filled another plate with ginger cookies. The kitchen was as cozy as the rest of the apartment was gracious, but touches like the traditional lace tablecloth from Ireland made it welcoming. "Safer than anywhere else in the world. That's why I wanted to show you the book from the capstone."

Elenda almost forgot about the horrifying reflection in the elevator. Almost.

"I'll try to get down there or have Dwight do it. How would a book make me safe?"

"No, dear, that won't do. It must be someone in the family, preferably you. No one who's not descended from Liam O'Dowd has ever opened our capstone. It won't happen for the first time on my watch. Honey or sugar?"

"On your watch?" Elenda shook her head. "Honey, please. I'm not following you, Gram. Why can't anyone open the capstone? Surely the city has to get down there for inspections or something."

"They do inspect the building, of course," she said, sitting down with the tea. "Though they'll never find one as well-built as this these days. But they don't get into the capstone. Or the vault."

"I've never even been in the vault. I don't much like the basement. Or the elevator."

"I do remember that, dear," her grandmother said. "I didn't like it when I was a girl, either. I outgrew that fear, as we all do. Tell me, have you kept up with your language studies?"

A sharp knock at the door startled Elenda badly enough that she almost dropped her teacup. She'd been about to ask this sweet old woman, one of her favorite people in the world, what the hell her years studying dead languages had to do with anything, or how some mysterious book could keep her safe. Her grandmother was up and opened the door before Elenda could even pick up her crutches.

"What a nice surprise! Two of my favorite people in one afternoon. Your father is joining us for tea, Lendy."

Elenda's father stepped inside, closed his eyes for a second, and sighed. Thomas Murphy was tall and rangy, his graying blond curls tamed by a business haircut. He'd already loosened his tie and unbuttoned his shirt. Unlike his wife, he wouldn't be caught dead wearing formal clothes unless he was forced to.

"Hey Mom. Thank goodness, Lendy. Dwight said you had a tough morning and handed me a pair of crutches. I was a little worried when I found your pain pills but couldn't find you."

"Sorry, Dad," Elenda said. She tried to stand to give him more room, but he put a hand on her shoulder and walked around to the other side of the table. "I just wanted some company."

"I'm glad you got that cast off," he said, adding milk to his own tea. "How long for the physical therapy?"

"Forever and a day. Depends on how much pain I can take."

"Well, you've beat things like this enough times. You'll come through with flying colors."

"I was just telling her she's a lot safer here," her grandmother said. "It's being away from home that lets these crazy things happen to any of us."

"I do fine when I'm working," Elenda said, winking at her father. They'd joked about her grace and good luck out in the wilderness compared to her klutzy tendencies elsewhere. "It's when I play it safe that I break bones."

"That makes perfect sense." Her grandmother nodded as she sipped her own tea. "It's where you live that counts. How was your day, Tommy?"

Elenda listened to the two of them chatter, trying to ignore the growing aches while remembering the odd things her grandmother said. Dementia didn't seem to run in the family, unlike the occasional youthful breaks with reality that everyone joked uneasily about.

A few of her cousins, only a handful out of a huge group scattered across the country, had succumbed to that madness before they'd turned forty. No one had ever been as old as her grandmother before it struck. But her Gram's words simply didn't make sense. Better to be safe than sorry.

When her father touched her shoulder, Elenda realized she wasn't hiding her physical or mental discomfort nearly as well as she thought.

"Thank you for the lovely tea, Mom," her father said. "I think someone's ready for those pain pills."

"You're right, Tommy, she's pale as a ghost. You get home and rest, Lendy, take care of your leg. Maybe when you're feeling stronger we can go down to the basement together."

Her father moved to help Elenda stand, but he was watching his mother.

"Anything I need to know about, Mom? Have you been feeling bad?"

"No, no, nothing of the sort. I'm just worried about my granddaughter. See you later."

Elenda remembered the portrait when the two of them passed by.

"Sorry about knocking this off," she said.

"Did you? It was on the wall when I got home, as usual." He grinned. "That thing's always falling off. No idea how it doesn't break into a million pieces, except Liam's insistence on keeping an eye on all of us."

The same huge foyer opened into her parents' apartment as her grandmother's, but almost everything else was different. Elenda detoured into the much larger, more modern kitchen to grab her pain pills, then took the quick hop down into the sunken living room. Her father followed a couple of minutes later with a glass of water and a whiskey for himself. He joined her on the silver and black sectional just as she arranged the pillows perfectly around, under, and behind herself.

She swallowed two of the pills, the kind she'd had right after the surgery that knocked her out in record time. She was willing to fall asleep now that someone was home. In fact, all she wanted to do was close her eyes and escape from her aching legs, the bizarre vision in the elevator, and all the rest for a little while.

Her father sorted through the absurd amounts of mail the Murphys got every single day, putting several neat piles in the usual place on her mother's desk. When he rejoined Elenda, he brought her back to her strange reality.

"You looked worried back there, at least until the pain got too bad. Something happen with your grandmother that I should know about?"

"You heard her talking about the vault in that awful subbasement," she said, yawning. "She seems to think something down there will keep me safe or something."

"Did she mention a book?"

"Yeah, she asked me about that on my birthday, too. I've never heard about any kind of a book, certainly not one hidden away like that. Do you know what she's talking about?"

Her father dropped his gaze, but he was smiling.

"I know the general idea, sure. I figured the time was coming. But that's not for me, Lendy. It never has been."

The pills were hitting Elenda like a solid black curtain. She'd taken them on a mostly empty stomach for that reason, but now she wished her thoughts were more clear.

"Now I don't understand what you're talking about, either."

"You will," he said. He covered her up to her chin with her favorite pink chenille blanket, kept out for this purpose since she'd returned. "Let me give you a rare bit of fatherly advice even though you're all grown up. Your grandmother's right. Focus on getting your leg stronger. You'll learn a lot from her when the time is right. There's no hurry at all now that you're home."

Elenda wanted to protest that she'd be leaving as soon as possible. She couldn't even force her eyes to stay open, her mouth to form words, her brain to make some kind of sense out of the past couple of hours.

She needed to... She had to ask her father another question. Again, something about that damn subbasement.

Opiates and exhaustion took it from her mind with the next breath.

# Chapter 6

Elenda tried her hardest to heed her father's advice to take it easy, relax, let her injuries sort themselves out. She knew she should listen to her doctors and to her slowly healing body. Another encounter with the elevator wiped out all of her best intentions barely a week later.

She'd tried riding with her eyes closed to avoid that mirror, window, whatever the hell it was. The low level nausea she always got with pain medication made that impossible, so Elenda stared at the wall, reading the less than reassuring safety instructions over and over.

Then the compulsion to look—to *know*—got the best of her.

The first reflection, on Monday, showed her with swollen and puffy eyes, wearing what was obviously a black dress of mourning. No sign of crutches, but all the signs of a devastating loss.

The next, before her Wednesday appointment, held a different angle, lower than the rest. Elenda sat in an elaborate, electronic wheelchair, her mother standing close behind.

The arrangement did not look or feel as temporary as yet another injury and slow recovery.

A motorized chair that expensive said forever.

The last reflection, on the way down this Friday morning, held herself still in the wheelchair, with her parents and Dwight behind her. The small car was crowded with her family's belongings. This time all their eyes showed signs of recent and prolonged tears.

After each vision, she thought of asking her grandmother or even her father about what she saw. And her fear of that fake smile she'd seen on her relatives' faces when her afflicted cousins came up in conversation kept her from saying a word.

Seeing that sickly sweet expression directed at her, about her, was more than she could stand to imagine.

When she returned from another painful PT session, Elenda convinced the driver she needed the walk with everything going so well. If the young man had been in that therapy room while Elenda trembled and sweated, he never would have agreed to let her out a block away. She moved as quickly as she could on the smaller crutches, the metal supports digging into her forearms.

Instead of heading to the main entrance and Dwight's protective gaze, she detoured down the cross street to the emergency exit. Compared to her recent habit of emailing her local friends and asking people at the hospital about short-term sublets, sneaking in the side door felt like a very small betrayal.

Some kind of change grew more important almost by the hour. Another three months of cowering in the elevator and avoiding her grandmother's odd requests would doubtless send her down the rabbit hole of insanity.

Her seldom-carried card key let her bypass the more public entrance, but rewarded her with an unplanned struggle to force the heavy steel door open. The stairwell that everyone, including the worried voice inside her own head, told her to avoid soared eight stories upward.

Pipes and wires, the building's life support systems, lined the concrete walls on two sides. The metal steps zigzagged against the other two, the handrails supported by steel uprights on the outside, anchored to the concrete on the inside. The vaguely chemical taste and smell of recent paint burned her eyes and lungs.

"Just take your time," she said under her breath. She held the right crutch under her left armpit. This part would certainly be easier without the longer version. "You've been up and down these a million times."

A million times. Yes.

With use of both legs, and with those legs conditioned to the task.

Elenda knew she'd made a mistake halfway up the second flight.

The problem wasn't only the strain of taking every step on one leg, already weakened from a long stretch of inactivity, then exhausted from her typical overzealous attack at physical therapy. It was more than her arms aching with the effort of pulling with her right and pushing with her left.

The problem was her balance. Every time she leaned on the crutch to lift her left leg, making sure not to put weight on her terribly weak right leg, she got more and more dizzy. Paint fumes amplified the effect. Her foot swung on an increasingly erratic pendulum, one that was eager to tip her backward and send her crashing down the dozens of concrete and steel ledges.

"Eleven more," she whispered, gritting her teeth, gripping the rail.

Elenda's heart pounded in her ears, and she smelled the oily sweat covering her body, increasing her chill in the cool stairwell. Turning around and going back down might be easier, but she was certain she'd lose her balance if she tried. She'd gone too far past her limits to reach her phone and call for help, even if she could get signal in this concrete tunnel.

Grunts with every step turned to groans.

Nine more steps.

Seven more.

Disaster struck three from the next broad expanse of concrete.

When she tried to force her exhausted thigh and hip muscles to drag her right leg up again, her toe caught under the lip of the step.

Pain from her wrenched knee tore through her. Elenda cried out, pulling her leg back, then screamed as her fragile balance deserted her.

She tried to grab the rail with her left arm, but the crutch caught on the step below and twisted her shoulder back. She landed hard on her left hip before tumbling down the stairs she'd so tortuously climbed, falling to the rock-hard landing.

She panted, too terrified to move. She'd fallen down stairs or off ramps or stages too many times to expect to be unhurt. But she'd been forced to remain still until an EMT could examine her neck and back many of those times as well.

If she'd managed to break a far more vital bone than she normally did, Elenda could do herself far more damage by trying to move on her own.

She was also one of the few residents who ever used these stairs, and had been for many years.

Her head had landed on her throbbing left shoulder, keeping her bruised skull from one more thump. She could see one of her crutches caught on the steps above, partly through the upright bars of the bannister. The other was under her ass. Sharp, jagged pain sang out from cuts and scrapes all over her face, arms, and hands. The impending bruises, especially on her hip, promised to be spectacular.

The rising stench of her own urine finally got her moving. She'd pissed herself on the way down.

Elenda turned her head forward as gently as she could, hissing at strained muscles in her neck and shoulders. Her arms and legs were screaming too loudly for her to have broken her back, and they reluctantly responded to her commands to move. Shifting enough to reach the crutch let her know she'd likely cracked at least one rib.

She pushed herself upright against the cold wall and waited for her heart rate and breathing to slow. She then pounded on the steel door with her crutch, resulting in a most satisfying and annoying hollow boom.

Her rescue came not long after from the third floor.

## Chapter 7

ELENDA WASN'T SURPRISED to see how her face looked in the hospital bathroom mirror when her parents picked her up the next day. The first unnatural elevator reflection had given her a lurid and detailed sneak-peak. The small diamond-shaped view hadn't revealed the reality of her strained neck and back, cracked ribs, and mild concussion.

"I don't understand what you were thinking," her mother said. "It could have been so much worse."

Elenda sat between them in the middle seat of the hospital shuttle, a young woman driving today. She hoped the usual driver hadn't been fired for letting her walk.

"I wasn't thinking anything, Mom. I just wanted to see if I could do it."

Marian turned to stare out the window, but not before blotting a tear with her monogrammed lace handkerchief.

As soon as the elevator in their building started moving, Elenda looked at the window. For the first time since she'd arrived, she saw only empty hallways followed by dark sections of floor. A hot, uncomfortable twist in her gut told her that didn't mean the whole bizarre ordeal was over.

Some sort of truce, fickle and brief, held sway.

When her mother turned right in her customary quick march toward their apartment, Elenda touched her father's shoulder.

"Dad, I have to ask you a really strange question. Keep in mind that I knocked myself silly yesterday."

"You sure did," he said, raising one eyebrow. "A performance you're not going to repeat. Hear me?"

She nodded, not the least bit upset by his gentle scolding. She deserved it, and probably more.

"I hear you, and I won't. Do you ever see a mirror in the elevator? In the little window?"

He took a deep breath and crossed his arms, leaning against the wall. Their multi-great grandfather loomed over his shoulder, frozen in time and eternal.

Instead of the fake cheer she was terrified of, her father's eyes were warm and a little sad.

"No, Lendy. I never have. It never worked that way for me."

She opened her mouth to speak before his words sunk into her medicated brain. Her stomach dropped even though she was standing on solid ground.

"For you?" she whispered. "Does it work that way for anyone?"

Her father smiled a little, then jerked his chin at the portrait.

"I understand it did for him, among other things. Sounds like it does for you, too."

"I don't understand anything anymore." Tears prickled Elenda's eyes and nose. "What does this mean?"

"It means you need to get settled and relax, let some of this sink in," he said. He matched her slow pace down the hall. "And that it's time for a nice, long talk with your grandmother. Soon as you're able. Agreed?"

"Agreed. She keeps saying I'll be safe here. If she can make that happen before I really do manage to break my neck next time, I'm ready to listen."

# Chapter 8

ELENDA'S BATHROOM mirror was as familiar and ordinary to her as her own hands. She'd stood on that cool white tile, mouth fresh from brushing her teeth or skin damp from taking a shower, seeing herself in the rectangular reflection on the back of the door as long as she could remember.

Her perspective had changed, certainly, from a toddler who had to reach up to hold the counter, to an awkward, skinny teenager who despaired of ever having curving hips or breasts like her mother, to the not as curvy as she'd hoped woman who nevertheless didn't usually mind catching a glimpse of herself in photos or reflection.

Yet today the view was as strange as anything she'd seen in the diamond-shaped version in the elevator.

Bruises decorated her flesh like algae blooming on a stagnant pond. Black and purple and green, all over her arms and legs. The worst were concentrated across her hips and back, along with the worst of the new pain. Dark clots of blood from scrapes highlighted several of the bruises and brought color to otherwise unmarked areas of her skin.

Underneath the deeper flashes of color were pale,

twisting scars contrasting with the dark red marks around her knee. Reminders of previous falls and surgeries. A living diagram of her life so far. And not every injury left a mark outside of her memory. Breaks healed with only a cast, sprains and strains that improved over time.

None of her accidents had ever happened in this building though. Even her grandmother had said she was safe here, and until a couple of days ago, she had been. Until she tried to make arrangements to move out again.

Her father seemed to believe whatever her grandmother wanted to tell her even though he wouldn't say what it was. That often-delayed trip to the subbasement finally felt more dangerous to avoid than to take. Elenda hoped to find out more about whatever secrets that damn elevator held as well.

She strapped the brace on her right leg, moving slowly to avoid hurting her cracked ribs. Her mother would have to help with her shoes, no way around that. But Elenda was relieved she didn't need help getting dressed today.

An hour later, a couple of the pain pills in her pocket just in case, she hobbled out into the hall just as her grandmother opened her door at the opposite end. Molly Murphy smiled, looking like a girl of eighteen about to set out on a great adventure. Elenda moved like an old, old woman to meet her underneath Liam's portrait.

"Oh sweetheart," her grandmother said, frowning when she got a closer look at Elenda. "My heart hurts to see you like this."

"Mine too, Gram. I hope we can figure out how to make it stop."

The older woman touched Elenda's arm.

"That will be up to you. Are you ready?"

"I don't know. I guess we'll find out."

Her grandmother took the brass skeleton key off the hook and slid it into the lock. She turned it to the right then pulled it back out. The down button glowed green instead of orange.

For the first time in over twenty years, Elenda wasn't afraid when she stepped into the elevator. The feeling of hot, clenching dread in her belly shifted to warm, fluttery excitement. This time her Gram turned the key a full rotation. All of the floor lights from the eighth floor to the basement turned red.

"How do we get to the subbasement?" Elenda said.

"Haven't you ever used the handle?"

"No, I was afraid to touch it."

"I was when I was your age. Now I think it's great fun."

The older woman pushed the handle forward, and the elevator dropped faster than it usually did. Elenda grabbed the rails, her crutches banging against the metal. She wasn't quite as fearless as she'd thought.

"I'm sorry, Lendy. I won't go quite so fast."

She winked, then eased back. Their descent slowed along with Elenda's heart. The chimes for each floor still sounded. She glanced at the window, hoping to see the empty floors. Her own face looked back, but all of the bruises and scrapes had vanished. She was tan and healthy, like she always was after leading a long hike or a ski trip. A secretive smile grew as she looked to her right. A tall, beautiful woman with stunning thick black hair stood beside her, her complexion a rich brown.

"Do you see things in the window, Gram?" As soon as the words were out, Elenda felt nearly as lightheaded as when her grandmother sent the elevator dropping like a rock.

"I used to." She glanced at the window, then turned back to Elenda. "When I was younger. I haven't seen anything but a window since your grandfather died."

Elenda closed her eyes, remembering the vision of herself in mourning clothes. Had she been seeing her

Gram's death? And she still didn't know *why* any of this was happening.

"What did you see then?"

"I saw myself smiling again." Elenda must have let her dismay show a bit too much. Her grandmother laughed. "That sounds awful, I'm sorry. I mean I saw that I wasn't going to cry forever. I still miss him every day, but that was the first time I understood I'd feel better eventually. I did, too. What do you see?"

"Nothing good," Elenda said. "Not until just a few minutes ago, but that's gone."

She wished for the strange mirror thing for the first time. Instead the window showed their slow progress past the lobby, sinking through the basement and a sea of glittering parked cars. A filthy and somehow frightening bunch of ancient pipes gave way to swirling layers of what looked like gray and white bedrock.

"How deep does this thing go, Gram?"

"Don't worry, Lendy. Neither of us is ready for the gates of hell. Not just yet."

## Chapter 9

As THE ELEVATOR coasted to a stop more gently than it ever did on the floors far above them, the rocky shaft opened up into a small room made of that same stone. When her grandmother let go of the handle, the door slid open.

Elenda could only see a couple of feet into the absolute darkness. If someone called the car back up, they'd be trapped down here in the pitch black deep below street level.

That was the first thing that scared her more than getting into the elevator in a long, long time.

"Are there any lights?"

"Of course," her grandmother said. "Do hold the door until I turn them on, though. Even these fancy modern bulbs don't last forever."

She stepped out onto a stone floor, rough but perfectly flat. She reached to the left of the door, and Elenda heard a soft click. Several beautiful curvy Art Deco glass fixtures flickered to life along the ceiling made of the same glittering gray rock as the floor and walls. Elenda suspected the bulbs were modern fluorescents, but those lovely green and black trimmed shades had to have been down here for a hundred years.

"What is this place? It's not the subbasement."

Her grandmother retrieved the key, and Elenda stepped out. The lights were controlled by two ancient round plastic cylinders, the one at the top now pushed in. She watched her Gram turn the key in yet another lock, one full turn to the right.

"We're below that, down in the family vault," she said. "You can step away from the door, dear. I have the elevator locked."

Elenda realized she was still holding her hand in front of the door. She followed her grandmother less than ten paces to the far end of the room carved deep into the Manhattan schist bedrock. Along the wall to their left, a narrow wooden table with a black leather top sat with four matching chairs. A gleaming solid brass door, as plain as most other fixtures in the building were ornate, covered the wall in front of them. An engraved oval doorknob waited over the final keyhole.

"This key opens only one door," her grandmother said with a smile.

She pulled a long, thick gold chain out of her blue sweater, a chain Elenda remembered her wearing on special occasions. At the end was a skeleton key made not of brass, but of the same gold. The top of the key was a cluster of red, blue, and white flowers surrounded by green leaves, the informal symbol many of her family wore in various kinds of jewelry. Elenda had a lovely enamel version made into a pin herself. She'd never seen it rendered in what had to be rubies, sapphires, diamonds, and emeralds.

Before Elenda could worry that the gold would be too soft, her grandmother fitted the key into the lock and turned it three times to the right. She grasped the handle and pulled. The door, almost the width of the wall, swung back.

Far from the mysterious hiding place Elenda was imagining, the light revealed rows of what looked like ordinary safe deposit boxes. The smaller ones had typical locks, and they were labeled with numbers. Several of those smaller ones a few inches tall clustered around a larger one in the middle, easily two feet square, again adorned with the cluster of flowers in gold set into the brass. This one had no lock.

When her grandmother touched the handle on that central drawer, every bit of Elenda's hair stood on end. She stepped back, letting go of her crutch to hold on to the table. Every cell in her body rose to full, uneasy alert.

The drawer opened smoothly, and Elenda's jaw dropped. A cylinder of pale green stone lay on black fabric in the middle, almost as thick as her wrist and nearly as long as her forearm. The smooth surface was covered with what she thought was ancient, archaic Irish, the various angled lines and dashes of the rudimentary alphabet. No wonder her Gram was asking her about keeping up with her language studies.

Ignoring the stone, her grandmother pulled out a leather book that had to be hand-bound. The stitches were neat and small, but more visible than in any factory-made book for well over one hundred years. This was covered in some kind of hide, smooth and dark brown as if it had passed through countless hands.

Pressed into that hide were ancient letters that confused Elenda for a second. She caught one shape, then another. She blinked as words older than the book moved into place in her mind.

"Legacy of the Land," she said in an airy voice.

"Exactly so," her grandmother said. She was beaming. "From the day you were born, I knew it would be you."

## Chapter 10

ELENDA SAT in the chair her grandmother pulled out, relieved to get off her leg even as her brain was spinning into mush. The green stone joined the book on the table.

"I don't understand," Elenda said, trying to steady her breathing. "Me for what?"

"Long before Liam O'Dowd left Ireland with his family, before he or his father or great-grandfather were ever born, a pact was made." Gram sat and picked up the stone wand. She turned it from side to side. Crystals and inclusions flashed and glinted among the carved markings. "Drawn between the people and the land. Only a few families under-stood the rewards, and the risks."

"What was the pact?"

Elenda kept her hands folded in her lap to keep from grabbing the stone. She was certain she'd be able to work out the symbols given enough time. She was even more certain that wasn't the way this ritual or ceremony or whatever was happening was supposed to go.

"One of the descendants must stay on the land," her

grandmother said. "As long as that happens, the family and the land will prosper."

"But we left Ireland."

"We did, and many millions besides us." Her grandmother put the wand down just out of reach and opened the book. She turned the pages carefully, but too fast for Elenda's rusty translation even as the primitive language shifted into Old Irish, then Gaelic. "The English didn't understand the bond between our families and the land they worked, or perhaps they didn't care to. When they decreed each plot would be divided among all the heirs, the promise was broken. And all fell into ruin."

The neat, close text on the thick vellum pages had given way to simple columns. The left column held a printed name, the right the same name signed and dated. Her grandmother turned a few pages before Elenda caught a date she could easily read.

"Is that the year 902? As in over a thousand years ago?"

"Some of these were copied from older scrolls and books, I believe," her grandmother said. "But the original signatures start well before our Liam and his family fled the great famine and starvation in 1849. He suffered as many did here, even after escaping Ireland."

"Then the building opened fifty years later."

"Liam and others of his generation learned how to survive, how to thrive in their strange new land." Gram was still turning pages, her finger tracing the signatures. "A handful of them had these stone wands, brought out at great risk to their families. The English damaged the magic, you see, but they could not destroy it."

"So the pact is with the building now?" Elenda said. Cold, hard chills ran all along her flesh, making the scrapes and bruises sing.

"The building and the bedrock all around us. You've been

to several of these in New York and in other cities. Each one has some sort of vault like this that holds the wand and the record."

"I'm sorry, Gram," Elenda said, shaking her head. Her stomach knotted as if she were in the elevator, still waiting for them at the other end of the room. "I still don't understand what this has to do with me. I don't seem to be safe here anymore."

She turned, taking Elenda's hand. She traced a scar on the back of her wrist, avoiding the fresh wounds.

"Did anything like this happen while you still lived here? Before you went to college?"

"No. It hadn't happened here before, either."

"I hope you'll forgive me for asking," her grandmother said, smiling. "Did you make plans to leave that day? Or try to?"

"How could you know that?" Elenda said. She fought the urge to pull her hand away. No one at the hospital would know who her grandmother was, much less have reason to pass along Elenda's casual inquiries about other places to live.

"I did the same thing a few times," her grandmother said. "My bad turns weren't as spectacular as yours, but the meaning was clear. Leaving here was a bad idea. If I had, none of the rest of the family would have been able to stay."

"What, am I on this list or something?"

## Chapter 11

Elenda's heart sped up as her grandmother turned the next page. The line of names stopped halfway down with Molly Donahugh Murphy and a flowery, looping signature. July 17, 1967.

"Not yet, Lendy. I wanted to tell you what I could first. Once your name appears, your fate is set."

"My *fate*?" Elenda pushed the chair back, the wood scraping across the stone, and picked up her crutches. "I'm not interested in being some kind of caretaker here. Dad loves this place. What about him?"

"The pact doesn't work that way," Gram said with a sigh. "We don't choose this place. This place chooses us. Sometimes I think that's part of the damaged magic. The building wants the ones who don't return the feeling."

"Well, I'm not going to sit around here and turn into some kind of throwback bitter old spinster."

But that image, the last one she'd seen. Elenda hadn't looked bitter. And that slow smile at the gorgeous woman beside her didn't exactly scream spinster. She'd never seen herself looking more healthy or happy.

"I wouldn't say I'm a spinster, dear," her grandmother said. Elenda was relieved she was smiling. "I had a thrilling life, before and after I settled here for good. I loved my life with your grandfather and our children. I had my work and traveled the world, much more than a lot of women my age did. I only had to return here when it was time to unpack. I grew to love living here over the years."

"What about those names?" Elenda pointed at the top of the page. "The ones that are crossed out? Did they get to make other arrangements? What are those dates?"

Her Gram's smile turned sad.

"They made other choices, the same as you're free to do. When they crossed their names out, another person took their place. The dates are when they died. All of them young. And all of them badly."

"You're not honestly telling me this damned building killed them?"

"I'm telling you the magic, the twisted, broken magic left by the English, upheld the pact. When they left, their immediate families went with them."

Elenda slumped in the chair, letting the crutches slip back to the floor. She'd seen that very thing, her parents leaving with their belongings.

And she'd seen herself in a wheelchair.

Permanently.

"So if I go..."

"The accidents will get worse, Lendy my dear," her grandmother said, tears in her eyes. "When I'm gone, your parents would have to leave as well. Probably before then. Something would happen to make it come about. A change in jobs, maybe another accident. One of your cousins would move into your place."

She took both of Elenda's hands. She tried not to flinch at her grandmother's soft touch on the scrapes on her palms.

"Don't test it again, please," her Gram said. "My heart breaks to see you hurt like this. I wouldn't be able to stand seeing you worse."

"My work, Gram," Elenda said. "I can't do what I love here. Not in the city. No one needs adventure sports here. They won't let me teach mountain climbing on the buildings, will they? Despite what my mother thinks, people aren't exactly lining up to learn ancient languages, either. I can't afford to live here even if I wanted to."

"No, you don't have to give that up. I never did. We traveled all over the world, sometimes for months. But this was always home. And the one listed in this book, bound by the pact, does not pay to live here. That's all laid out in a very modern contract on file in the building manager's office. This situation is not without its rewards to make up for your sacrifice."

"Sacrifice is right," Elenda said. She drew away from the table, not wanting to touch the book or the stone. "How do you even know it's me? Just because you want it to be?"

"I do want it to be, yes, because I see how much pain you're in. But I'd never wish this on anyone who wasn't ready. I can't override what the building wants. I can't overpower the pact. You told me earlier you see visions in the elevator window."

"I do, or I did. But I don't understand how that leads some kind of life sentence to stay here. One I did not choose or agree to."

"There's more than that, my dearest. You still have a choice, but not an easy one."

Her grandmother gestured toward the book, toward where the names stopped with her own. Or where they had.

Elenda's blood ran hot, then cold at the faint lines appearing on the page. The tall capital letters first, and she couldn't deny the E taking shape no matter how badly she wanted to.

"I can't do this, Gram," she said, pulling herself up out of the chair. She managed to keep from groaning. Her abused and sore muscles had gotten stiff in the cool air. "I love you, and I appreciate you trying to help. But this is beyond what I can handle."

"You can think it over, of course. All I ask is that you be careful, Elenda. I don't want you to have an even worse accident. There wasn't a whole lot of room to play with after this last one, was there?"

"Do you realize how you sound?" Elenda said, dismayed at how quickly she was furious. "You're telling me if I don't follow some ancient spell I'm not even allowed to read, this building will somehow kill me?

"I know exactly how it sounds," her grandmother said. She gazed steadily at Elenda, but she made no move to get up and join her. "My grandfather told me the same things, and I thought he was just as crazy. He admitted thinking his own mother was a loon when she told him. But all of us recognized the truth over time."

"And your reward was long and healthy life, right? And the ones who resisted didn't live long enough to tell the tale."

Elenda grimaced at the harsh and angry sound of her own voice, amplified by the stone walls. Her grandmother didn't deserve to be talked to like that. And yet she couldn't seem to stop herself.

"I can't say you have years and years to make your choice, Lendy. But nothing has to be decided right this second. I just dumped a lot into your mind. I'm sorry."

"No, I'm sorry, Gram," Elenda said, shaking her head. "I'm being awful to you. Whatever this is really about, you're only trying to help me. Come on, Mom will be worried about us."

The older woman replaced everything in the bizarre safe and closed the massive door. She turned the lights out, hiding all of the mysteries from sight. At least for a little while.

Elenda hoped forever, even though she knew in her aching bones that wasn't true.

## Chapter 12

A COUPLE of hours and a couple of pain pills later, Elenda waited in the small family dining room for her father to get home. Her mother had banished her from the kitchen, a place she was uncomfortable in under the best of circumstances. The crutches and her slow and awkward movement were too much for either of them to handle.

Her phone vibrated in her pocket, and for some reason a chill raced through her. This anxiety wasn't as simple as not wanting to be scolded for devices at the table like a teenager, or as complicated as an unwelcome message from one of her various exes.

This chill began and ended with the lingering pains in her body and her heart, both new and old.

Elenda's smile at hearing from one of her oldest friends faded with every line.

Sorry she didn't get back sooner. Yes, there is a sublet opening up, less than a mile away. Closer to the hospital. Short term lease no problem for a grade school hiking buddy.

And of course, Elenda had to decide right away. Within

twenty-four hours, before the place went on the market. She put the phone on the table, then covered her face in her hands.

Right on time, as if her Gram had planned it that way.

Disgusted at such a nasty thought, she grabbed the phone and tapped out a quick reply. She hit the send button before she could change her mind.

Asking how much and what floor it was on couldn't possibly hurt a thing.

Another hour passed before she heard another phone ringing in the kitchen. Her mother had been back and forth several times, wondering and worrying what was taking Elenda's father so long. After a few minutes of quiet conversation, Marian joined her daughter at the table. Her face was pale and strained.

"What's wrong, Mom?"

"Everything's fine, Lendy." The lie could not possibly have been more obvious. "Your father will be home in a few minutes."

She refused to say more.

When Elenda's father finally came in, more than two hours late, he was a different man than the one who'd left that morning. His step was slow and heavy, and his face was nearly as pale as his wife's.

After a couple of minutes in the kitchen, the two of them joined Elenda at the table. Her mother's lashes were damp, her eyes red and puffy.

Elenda struggled to keep her face straight while her thoughts raced.

This is all my fault. Whatever it is, illness or some other disaster, this is all because I'm too stubborn to do what my grandmother wants me to do. I'm too stubborn to have a damn permanent address, no matter what it costs me or anyone else.

"Listen, I'm not sure this is going to come to anything," her father said. His voice and drooping shoulders said otherwise. "I may be getting transferred to our West Coast division."

"They swore this wouldn't happen, Tom," Elenda's mother said, tapping her fingers on the dark oak table. "Years ago. It's supposed to be in your contract."

"It is there, Marian. And sometimes these mergers get more complicated than we expect."

"Not permanently, right?" Elenda said. "Just for a transition or something?"

"I'm afraid not. If this thing goes through, our whole team goes. Most of them are even excited about it."

"And you're not, Dad."

It wasn't a question. The only question was whether Elenda could live with this any longer than she lived through another series of accidents.

"No, I'm not. I fought to get that into my contract for a reason." He took his wife's hand as he looked around the small room. Unlike the larger formal dining room, this one was lined with family photos and mementos. "I don't want to leave the city. I don't want to leave our home."

"I'm sure you can fight it," Marian said, a flash of color returning to her cheeks. "People don't have to just take these things anymore. You have options."

"Yeah, I suppose I do," he said. He scrubbed his fingers through his hair, leaving it standing in disorganized gray and blond peaks. "Not many good ones at my age, though."

"This will break Gram's heart," Elenda said, almost to herself.

"I'm worried about that too," her father said. "She's doing well, sure. But things like this aren't easy on young people, much less someone her age. Did you two get a chance to talk today?"

Elenda stared at her father, wishing she could transfer this whole thing to him. Let him be the one the building wanted. The one the damned pact wanted.

Even a line through her own name, through her own life, wouldn't make that happen.

"We did talk," she said, wiping tears away before her parents saw them. "I'd like to talk to you, though. Mom, too. Maybe not right now."

Elenda's mother placed her hands flat on the table, then got to her feet.

"I think this is the perfect time for you to talk," she said. She touched Elenda's shoulder, then her father's. "I'll get dinner warmed up."

**Chapter 13**

ELENDA WATCHED HER MOTHER LEAVE. The radio in the kitchen clicked on, then got louder than Marian usually kept it. Pop music from Elenda's teen years, her mother's guilty pleasure known only to the three of them, created a fast-paced wall of privacy. When Elenda met her father's gaze, his eyes didn't look any less upset, but he was smiling.

"We don't have to do this now, Dad."

"We're both sitting right here. Your mother's making it clear she thinks it's time." He crossed his arms and leaned back in his chair, long legs stretched under the table. "I've never been more desperate for a change of subject."

A short bark of laughter, manic and strange, escaped Elenda's tight throat.

"It may not be a change of subject, not if Gram was telling me the truth." She drew in a shaky breath. "What do you know about the family vault? Down in the subbasement?"

Her father half smiled, raising his eyebrows.

"I know we have a bunch of paperwork in one of the deposit

boxes down there. Wills, deeds, a few stocks. Nothing we need to get to all that often, but things I'd rather have here than at the bank. I've never seen inside the big safe, Lendy, if that's what you're asking. I'm guessing your Gram showed you that today."

"Yeah, she did." Elenda ran her hands through her hair just before she realized she shared that habit with her father. "Am I... Does it break some kind of secret rule if I talk to you about this?"

"If it does, your grandmother and her grandfather before her broke that rule a long time ago. Bunch of the cousins did, too. I heard the tales of the book, the legacy book. She told me I'm not in there, no matter how much I always wanted to be. Still true?"

"Still true. I wish you were instead of me. Is this why you might get transferred, Dad? Because of me?"

He shrugged.

"This is where your grandmother might know more, but I doubt she does. No one seems to have all the answers, at least no one alive. Her theory on why you keep getting hurt is because you resisted the fate you were born to. Does that make sense to you?"

Elenda rubbed her aching eyes.

"Well, the timing fits, anyway. I'd asked around about sublets before I had my little accident in the stairwell. Earlier that same day. Then today, after Gram took me down to the vault, I heard back about one. As soon as I replied and said I was interested, you called Mom."

"If anyone else told me that, anyone outside the family, I wouldn't believe a word of it. But coming from you, and about this, I'm afraid to *doubt* a word of it."

He sat forward and took one of Elenda's hands into his own cold ones.

"This isn't something you can be forced into, Elenda. I

don't think it works that way, but even if it did, I'd never want that."

"What if it is why you're getting transferred? You wouldn't want—"

"No. I would not. I doubt my mother agrees with me, but I would much rather you make your own choices, live your own life, instead of making yourself miserable staying here."

Elenda surprised herself by smiling.

"Gram said the building wants the ones who don't want to live here. Like a cat knowing which person does not want a lapful of cat hair."

"That's just what I've always heard, but not put so well. We all talked among ourselves, long before we understood what we were talking about. The cousins, nieces, nephews. Everyone who wasn't chosen, the ones who were. Some like me who wanted this, others who were scared to death it would be them."

"Like me," Elenda whispered.

"Maybe so. I think my generation got a lot more quiet and secretive before any of you were born. You didn't have a bit of warning, did you?"

"Not even a hint. Not until Gram started asking me about the vault."

"I'm sorry about that, sweetheart, I truly am. I don't know why all of us changed at once. Maybe paranoia about causing bad luck somehow. Maybe fear of the government finding out and making us pay taxes or something. You know all that conspiracy theory nonsense that went around back then. Hell, maybe something to do with our whole culture changing, people moving around so much more than they used to. Whatever the cause, it wasn't fair to you or anyone else your age."

"Oh, I don't know. If I had known, do you think I

would have ever come home? You might not have seen me a single time after high school."

"Listen, seriously, don't make a decision you're going to regret. Not because of me, and not because of your grandmother."

"You know what else Gram said, Dad? She said that was why I get hurt so much, why my accidents keep getting worse. Did she tell you about the people who did decide to ignore all of this and leave anyway? What happened to them?"

He closed his eyes and turned away.

"I went to their funerals. Visited a couple in facilities. I never knew for sure, but we all suspected how they got that way. *Why* they got that way. I'm sure she showed you the book. I'd be willing to bet the crossed out names match up with all those early deaths, or the ones who lost their minds."

"So you know what could happen to me. Choice or not, this truly is life or death." Elenda waited until her father looked back at her and nodded. "How much does Mom know about all of this?"

"Only the general idea. How someone in the family always stays with the building, just like on the land that's left back in Ireland. She knows it's not me, but that because it is my mother, our rent is a tenth of what anyone else would pay. I don't have to tell you how much she loves living here. For what it's worth, though, she wouldn't want you to be forced into anything, either."

Elenda gazed around the room, at the photos all over the walls. Mostly of her and her parents, though her grandmother was in quite a few. She couldn't imagine any of them living anywhere else, not any more than she'd ever seen herself living here for the rest of her life.

She hadn't imagined living here even one more day after she left for college with no intentions of looking back.

"I don't know how to make a decision like this, Dad. I never really have, you know? The longest lease I ever signed was six months, and I hated the place from that day until I got away. Even that's longer than my longest relationship."

Her father snorted softly, smiling at the same time.

"That part I can't help you with. I have no doubt you'll meet the right person when you're ready." He let go of her hand, sat back, and sighed through his lips. "I can't really help you with the rest, either. I want you to be safe, sure. It rips my heart out to see you hurt like this. I want you to be happy, too."

"Back to square one." Elenda smiled to soften her words. "Does all this new secretiveness mean you don't know anyone my age who's signed on for this? Someone I could talk to?"

"I have my suspicions. This is another question for your grandmother, Lendy. I don't know if anyone keeps central records or anything like that, though it would make sense. I'm sure she knows everyone else in the city. Probably all along the East Coast. I wouldn't be surprised if she knew a lot more."

Elenda nodded, wondering if her grandmother would only give her names of people who were happy with the arrangement. When the radio in the kitchen snapped off, she jumped hard enough to cause a knotting spasm through her wrenched back.

If the next fall would be worse than this, anything her grandmother said, anyone Elenda talked to, may not make any difference.

## Chapter 14

THE VAST CAFETERIA-STYLE restaurant in the East Village was less crowded than usual in the brief hours between the lunch and dinner rushes. Elenda had arrived earlier than she meant to. The mostly Eastern European staff didn't mind to hold the table, happy to have a chance to slow down and chat with her. Colorful murals decorated the walls, and Old World comfort food and a dizzying variety of pastry waited to settle the nerves fluttering around in her belly.

As soon as Elenda's grandmother had given her the list, much longer and covering far more of the world than her father suspected, the decision of who she most needed to talk to was clear. Her cousin Rick lived down in Washington, DC, where he was born, but he and his family had often visited New York when he and Elenda were young. She remembered a moody, distant boy who never seemed to fit in.

Her youthful self couldn't resist the challenge of another outsider, and the two became close friends. Elenda hadn't seen Rick for a while, but she'd heard stories about his rising and falling fortunes. Some of those stories included treatment for serious depression, but not for a few years now.

Elenda knew her old friend would tell her the truth. Rick cooperated by immediately agreeing to take the train up for a visit.

She recognized him as soon as he walked in the door. The skinny, pale boy with thick glasses and floppy brown hair had vanished along with the gaunt, shadowed look of his teenaged years. Rick exuded comfort in the space around him, in his clothes, in his skin. The handsome man who lit up the room with his smile when he saw Elenda had moved beyond finally fitting in. Rick now had a deep, natural confidence that spread to everyone around him.

"You look fantastic, Lendy, crutches and all!"

"Well, better than I did a few weeks ago for sure." Elenda ignored the metal appendages and she stood just in time for his hug. "You look wonderful, Rick. Something's been treating you right."

He rolled his eyes and shook his head, a habit Elenda remembered well.

"I think maybe I finally grew up. Happens to all of us if we live long enough. Now tell me how the hell you broke yet another bone, cousin?"

The catch-up talk lasted through a delicious and generous Ukrainian meal and decadent round of sweets before Elenda ran out of time. She'd almost managed to convince herself this was nothing but a long-overdue visit, or maybe a successful young writer gathering material for a comedic story about her spectacular run of bad luck. Not a far more sinister interview about a topic she was afraid made her sound crazier than it made her feel.

Rick was gentle about it, but he yanked her back to reality quite effectively.

"So I hear through the usual channels that you may be rejoining us on the East Coast?" he said, one eyebrow raised.

"And what channels are those?" Elenda tried not to laugh, but it was a losing battle. "I haven't decided anything just yet."

"You already talked to Auntie Kay, my dear Lendy. You know she didn't want someone else to scoop her with news that big."

This time it was Elenda's turn to roll her eyes.

"What does she have, some kind of phone tree set up?"

"Something like that. She might even have her own app by now. Listen, I'd be the last one to dig into your business if you don't want me to. I know you called me for a good reason. I have a good idea what it is, too, but I want you to tell me."

Elenda let out a long breath through pursed lips. She'd almost forgotten how direct and no nonsense Rick could be. Again, exactly what she needed to get herself talking in a case like this.

"If you talked to Auntie Kay you already know why, don't you?" He shrugged, leaving her no choice but to spill it. "My grandmother, she's not sick or anything, but she's been talking to me about where I might want to live next. Or where I might have to, if I know what's good for me for a change."

Rick nodded slowly, not quite smiling.

"Sounds familiar. That's pretty much how it finally hit me. Only I didn't have your habit of collecting broken bones. I was well on the way to breaking my mind, though."

"When you lived somewhere else, right?" Elenda said, the hair on her arms standing up. "But when you went back home, it got better?"

"Exactly right. I'm not sure if our family is lucky or cursed. No one tells us we're wasting our time with jobs like writing or leading extreme outdoor adventures or all the other weird things we get into. But if some of us decide to move out on our own, all hell breaks loose."

Elenda watched his brown eyes, afraid to interrupt now that he was talking. Her Auntie Kay had been all positive and excited, full of nothing but stories of how wonderful her life was. How wonderful Elenda's life would be once she got settled in.

Just as Elenda had suspected, Rick's experience sounded a lot more like her own.

"I'm sorry to drag all of this up," she said. "I just...I wanted someone to be honest with me instead of trying to sell me on the idea, you know?"

"I do know. I'll tell you the truth whether you really want it or not, on one condition."

"Name it."

"If you do decide to stay on this side of the country, we don't go ten years between visits ever again."

Elenda laughed, more tension than she'd realized leaving her body in an instant. Even if all of it came right back, she was grateful for the reprieve.

"You got it. You can stay with me, and my grandmother will spoil you stinking rotten."

"I'll hold you to that. I could use a good dose of Molly's spoiling." Rick waited for the waiter to refill both of their teacups, staring at Elenda the whole time. He didn't speak until she nodded.

# Chapter 15

"So I GET out of college, all prepared to write my Great American Novel. Or at least the novel that sold a ton of copies. You already know that first one *did* sell well. Probably too well. Once I started seeing steady income and got a contract for the next two, what was my gift to myself?"

"You moved to New York. Just like writers are supposed to."

"Of course. That was almost a requirement of the book deal. And everything gradually fell to pieces. I got the next two books out, yeah. The few people who read them raved about how much better they were than the first. And no one else bought them. Not until some asshole decided to claim the third one as his own."

"I'd forgotten about that! I was already out West collecting those broken bones. You ended up in court for a while, didn't you?"

Rick picked up his heavy white tea mug, turning it between his hands and breathing in the bergamot-scented steam.

"Three years with all the paperwork and continuations

and nonsense. Long enough to eat up everything I'd earned and send me down into the pit inside my head for even longer. He finally tripped himself up when they forced him to testify, but the damage was done. I knew I'd never plagiarized a word from him or anyone else, and he finally had to admit it. That wasn't nearly as exciting a story, though, so not many other people heard the outcome.

"I moved back home to get my head on straight, and to try to get out of the financial mess. I hadn't written much during all that time. Partly paranoia about another lawsuit, justified or not. Mostly depression. I assumed moving back into the same old building in the same old city I'd grown up in would put me in the hospital, but I didn't see any other choice. Just the opposite happened. I was writing, feeling better, and even those first three novels started selling again."

"Miracle cure, huh?" Elenda said. "I heal up so fast here that the doctors can't believe it. At least until I manage to fall down a few flights of concrete steps."

Rick winced, closing his eyes for a second.

"You know, I've thought several times I'd give anything to have this affect my body instead of my mind. It would suck just as bad, wouldn't it? Anyway, when my fourth novel came out, all was forgiven. They were talking TV pilots, maybe a movie. So what did I do again?"

"Same thing I did, of course. Finally move out on your own so you can start your life."

"Like normal people, right?" Rick's voice was low, bitterness making Elenda's heart ache. "That was the biggest joke of all from the day we were born. That time my great escape was heading out to Los Angeles. I figured a real change of scenery would do me good. When all the deals fell through, I ended up in the psych ward for a couple of months. Want to guess what happened next?"

Elenda shook her head. She didn't want to guess, and she

really didn't want to hear more. And this kind of tale, once started, had to be finished.

"Same thing that happened to me not that long ago," she said. "Your parents wanted to take care of you and help you recover, so back you went."

"They really were great. My parents, I mean. They weren't trying to force me into anything either way. My mother knew the history of crazy floating around our gene pool as well as we all do. And I did recover. Even got a couple of novellas and a bunch of short stories out into the world."

"What kept you from heading out into the world again?"

"My own version of your grandmother. My grandfather caught me aside when I started talking about moving. I think my mother clued him in. To tell you a truth I haven't admitted to anyone else, I was already pretty clear on the pattern, and terrified that I'd never be able to break out of it. So I was ready to listen."

He picked at the remains of poppy seed cake.

"I'm not saying I regret my decision. These last seven years have been the best of my life in a lot of ways. But I do wish I'd been a bit more clear-headed when I made it. I've been through anger at my mother, my grandfather, and most of all myself for not taking the time to truly understand what I was doing. I also knew if I waited, if I instead decided to test the depths of my lurking insanity, that I probably wouldn't make it out at all.

"So I signed the little book in the basement, probably a hell of a lot like the one you've seen by now. I can't say I've never looked back or wondered what would have happened if I'd left anyway, but I'm still there." He tapped his temple. "And I'm still here."

"Do you ever wonder what would happen if you did change your mind, Rick? If you just decided to move out even after you signed?"

"Don't have to wonder." He smiled, but it was tight and humorless. "A few people have done just that. The last a couple of years ago in Chicago. Her name was Cassie. Most of them have killed themselves within a few months. A few have been locked up for good. Cassie did both and managed to off herself in the hospital."

Elenda rubbed her eyes with both hands, squeezing until purple lightning filled her vision. Her eyeballs ached and the afterimage lingered when she met Rick's gaze.

"So you're telling me to-"

"No no, none of that. All I'm telling you is what happened to me. Our family is actually a good bunch despite our unique situation of luxurious indentured servitude. But you're one of my favorites even in a mostly likable group. I'd be sad if something worse happened to you, Elenda. But I'd respect your decision no matter what. I respected Cassie even though I knew what would happen. Partly because she did too, and she did it anyway."

He leaned forward and lowered his head, looking up into Elenda's eyes.

"All I'm telling you is make sure you know what you want. Don't rush into anything. This legacy had us maybe before we were born, but once you sign that book, it's for life. A very long life, too, judging by everyone I've met since I joined the club. So *make sure.*"

Elenda watched a group sitting nearby, all of them speaking a language she couldn't understand. Those words sounded as odd to her ears as the ancient Irish and other languages she knew would sound to almost everyone else in the city. They'd possibly left home and family behind with no real expectation of ever seeing them again.

New York was full of people who'd fled awful situations Elenda didn't want to imagine.

All that uncertainty, fear, and sacrifice for the chance at a new life.

The same thing Liam O'Dowd had given her family over a hundred years ago.

"Do you have a portrait in your building, Rick? The first one from your family who left Ireland?"

"You mean our Eternal Hall Monitors?" He snorted. "They're there, sure. A floor below mine, but close enough. Robert and Katharine Sullivan were more all-seeing than Santa to my young self. I remember yours, opposite that creaky old elevator, right?"

"One of the reasons I never much liked that elevator. Liam O'Dowd knows exactly who comes and goes, probably in the whole building. Listen, Rick, do you have to get back right away? Or can you stay for a couple of days? I have a thousand questions, if you're willing. And I'll be selfish and admit I just want to talk to someone my own age about all of this."

Rick's smile erased her pain and confusion, and years of his own fell away from his face. They were two weird kids hiding out from all the normal people all over again.

"Ask me anything you can think up, cousin." He leaned forward, looking into her eyes and grinning like the devil himself. "Do you have any idea how many times I've wanted to rewrite all of this for myself? How rarely anyone actually *gets* that chance? I'll do anything in my power to make sure this is on your own terms, for your own reasons. Then I'll toast your success and independence no matter what you decide. Deal?"

## Chapter 16

ELENDA DIDN'T FEEL the chill, in the air or in her bones, nearly so much the next time she stood beside her grandmother in the family vault. Several people joining them warmed up the bedrock space more than she expected. A couple of weeks passing had let her body heal enough to not be nearly so achy and sore.

The main difference was the warmth in her heart. A settled, secure warmth. She didn't quite trust that sensation, one she'd never felt here or anywhere else in her entire life. But she enjoyed the solid comfort nonetheless.

The short crutches waited in the corner beside the elevator, but Elenda was relieved to stand on her own as her grandmother opened the massive vault door once again. Rick stood with her Auntie Kay and another cousin she'd spoken to in a row behind her, her father on Rick's other side.

Their words and stories of how their lives had changed since they'd accepted the legacy of the family land wouldn't have been enough to change Elenda's mind on their own.

Not if all of them had been glowing and positive, anyway. Physical, financial, emotional, none of the mysterious incentives were exactly the same. Elenda didn't doubt the challenges they told her of were true, though, and exactly what would be most effective in every case.

None of them were dressed formally by New York City standards, but blue jeans and t-shirts had no place on a day like this. Elenda wore a dark blue ankle-length dress that coordinated with her grandmother's pale blue suit. The older woman turned slowly, holding the heavy green stone wand as if it were light as a feather. Eyes bright and cheeks glowing, she looked at least twenty years younger.

"Elenda Margaret Murphy. The land has need of a steward. A protector. One to watch over and provide for. An exchange of love and sacrifice."

Elenda's grandmother stepped forward, still holding the stone close to her body.

"That sacrifice demands a choice, though it offers great reward. You must choose freely. You must understand the seriousness of the bond you make with magic older than the country we call home."

"I understand," Elenda said. "I choose freely and with my own will."

"Then, my dear granddaughter, we welcome you."

Elenda took the wand carefully, surprised at how warm it felt. The heat didn't come from her grandmother's hands, not with the whole length and breadth of green rock as long as her own forearm. That much warmth could only come from within.

Her grandmother turned back to the vault and brought out the leather-bound book. She opened it on the table, turning the page to the last line of signatures and dates. Elenda wasn't at all surprised to see her own name fully formed.

"As you must choose with your own mind and heart,"

her grandmother said, "you will sign with your own hand. As it has been since time too distant to measure."

Elenda was confused when her grandmother pulled an ordinary black ballpoint pen out of her breast pocket. A rather nice Cross model, of course, no disposable junk for Molly O'Dowd Murphy. But none of the long, arching ostrich plumes, solid gold fountain pens, or dire instruments for extracting her blood that she'd imagined.

The older woman winked when Elenda shifted the stone wand to her right hand and took the overwhelmingly normal writing instrument. She stepped back, leaving Elenda alone with the book.

Sudden trembling threatened to overwhelm her still-weak legs. Elenda sat, closing her eyes to let a thousand questions flash through her mind. More than a thousand, and more than her own lifetime's worth.

But for her, and in this lifetime, all of the questions came down to only one answer. One she never would have believed even a few short days ago, but now Elenda made the decision for herself, free and clear.

As she formed the swirls, lines, and angles of her own name, the settled, comfortable warmth moved out from her heart. Her belly, her throat, her legs, even her fingers took on the inner glow.

The sensation was strongest in her left hand, curled over the stone wand on the table beside her. A sharp, high scratching, heard more with her fingertips than with her ears, kept pace with the softer scratch of pen across paper. Elenda's left palm grew hot enough that she was afraid she'd have a blister to go with all the rest of her healing wounds, but she kept her hand still.

The stillness felt right, somehow.

Elenda put the pen down and raised her left hand at the same moment. On the paper to her right, the date took shape beside her signature, black letters floating up from the pale surface.

On the wand, a far more primitive signature glowed before shifting to the same paler green of the other markings. A flat line like a table, with five diagonal lines underneath. Elenda didn't recognize that word, not from the original artifacts, anyway. She knew if she studied the stone, though, perhaps compared with the signatures above her own in the ancient book, she'd find more breadth and depth to the primitive language than she or any other scholar had suspected.

She got almost gracefully to her feet and turned right into the arms of her grandmother.

"Welcome, my dearest, my darling girl," she whispered. "The land welcomes you home."

**Chapter 17**

LATER THAT SAME DAY, Elenda couldn't stop staring at the view from her new apartment. Even in a building she'd lived in or come home to throughout her life, she'd never suspected a vista so custom-made for her own eyes, mind, and heart.

The trees, grass, water, and stone of Central Park didn't take up the whole horizon, but the stretch she could see was enough to settle her wanderlust for the moment. Even with a crowd swirling behind her on the huge patio space, when Elenda leaned her elbows against the gray stone pillar and focused on the park, she could pretend no one else was anywhere around her.

Behind her, several strides away from the edge of her outdoor paradise, the building rose straight up to the roof, with the setback giving her nearly as much room outside as in. The previous tenant had taken advantage of the space and the sunlight with several garden boxes scattered around the area.

Almost all of them were empty now with autumn coming on and the family leaving, but Elenda thought she would continue the garden herself. With room for climbing plants against the building and several other levels and arrangements all around her, growing her own food could be another way of making herself at home.

A soft footstep behind her brought Elenda back to the reality of ignoring her own apartment-warming party. She picked up her drink and turned to rejoin the festivities.

"This is a beautiful view," her mother said. "I'd never been down here before you decided to move in."

Marian wore her usual dark blue pantsuit, but she'd added a scarf and jewelry in the same lighter shades as Elenda and her grandmother wore. The choice of apartment wasn't one she approved of, and she'd worked very hard to keep that to herself. Elenda gave her mother full credit for what had to have been a difficult effort. Even with the reality of none of the top floor family apartments being available, she knew her mother thought she should just live at home until one opened up.

"I had no idea you could see the park from here," Elenda said. She inspected the garden and flower boxes, some still vibrant with greens and colorful autumn flowers. "I think I may have to take up gardening, believe it or not. Maybe you can help me figure out what to do with this stuff once I grow it."

Their eyes met, and both women smiled. Elenda knew in her heart that the one floor separation between them would make all the difference in the world, in the best way.

"Nothing brings more joy to a city dweller's heart than fresh produce and flowers." Elenda's mother ran her finger-tips through a tight bundle of deep red mums. "I'm sure we can work out what to do with anything you grow."

The setback between floors was deep enough to let about twenty people wander around, with a few more sitting inside the nearly empty apartment. Several family members who hadn't been part of the ceremony had joined them for the late afternoon party, almost like a wedding reception after the service.

Elenda laughed under her breath, thinking this situation wasn't all that different.

"I could use a little help looking for furniture, too," she said. "I've never had much more than would fit in a few suitcases."

Her mother's eyes lit up, and she tilted her head.

"Well, we have plenty down in storage, but you already know that. If any of it suits you, it's yours. Otherwise we'll find exactly the pieces you love most."

Delia, one of Elenda's friends who'd been on that life-altering - and knee-shattering - trip to Colorado, broke away from the group in front of the open door. When Elenda started to wave her friend over, her mother grabbed her hand. Before Elenda processed her surprise at such an impulsive action from proper Marian Murphy, her mother's words drove it from her mind.

"Nothing on earth would make my heart happier than to have you home, Elenda. But I don't want your heart broken. Are you sure about all of this? Are you happy?"

"I'm not sure about anything. This whole thing hasn't give me much time to think, not that too much time to think ever works out well for me. I am happy, Mom. I didn't miraculously turn into a homebody overnight, no. Being back in the city will take some getting used to. But I'm happy."

The two women hugged tight, and Elenda kissed her mother's cheek.

"That's all I need to hear," Marian said. "Welcome home."

A stubborn irritation in her eyes, very much like tears, kept Elenda blinking furiously. She watched stuttering stop motion as her mother turned away, paused to hug Delia, and kept moving. By the time Delia's dark brown streaked with purple hair swam into view, Elenda had herself more or less under control.

"Quite the setup you have here, Ms. Murphy. No room-mates, either?"

"No one at the moment. It is nice not to be desperate and begging someone to move in for a change."

Delia turned in a slow circle, her bright blue eyes taking in every detail as they had since the two of them met on a grade school hiking trip. One of the good things about moving back to the city would be visiting more friends scattered across the boroughs rather than across the country. Delia's message about a sublet close to the hospital, and the almost immediate call from Elenda's father, had set countless unseen wheels in motion.

"I'm not even going to ask what kind of crater this place made in your bank account," Delia said. "I've never known you to even have a year-long lease, and now you own a view several million people would kill for."

Both women leaned against the just over waist high stone wall facing the park.

"It wasn't as bad as you'd think, Dee. I'm sure I'll take a while to get used to the city again, but I think this will make a good home base."

Delia leaned forward, wavy hair falling into the breeze. Elenda hoped she'd eventually come to trust the compact she'd made with the land and the wand as much as she trusted the iron-clad but ordinary contract she'd signed in the business office. Even if her physical accidents stopped, she doubted she'd ever have the same dancer's confidence as her friend. Delia rose to her toes, shoulders pushed far past the boundary.

Right before Elenda gave up her struggle to keep from

yanking her friend onto more solid footing, Delia straightened, flipped her hair back, and caught Elenda in a quick hug.

"I say you've had more than enough bad luck over the years, Lendy. If coming home changes all of that for you, maybe that tumble back in Colorado was worth it."

## Chapter 18

**Three months later**

CLIMBING out of a taxi with no help at all - from crutches, leg braces, or another person - was a miracle Elenda was determined to remember. Even after three glorious weeks of summertime mountain climbing in Chile, stepping out onto a freezing New York City sidewalk under her own power delighted her. Dwight's broad smile only reinforced how much progress she'd made over the past few months.

"You look great, Lendy," he said. The junior doorman was already gathering her bags to take upstairs. "Had a good trip?"

"Fantastic trip, Dwight. I finally feel like myself again."

"Well, you look like a million bucks. Glad to see you home safe and sound."

Elenda tried to keep her rueful smile to herself as she walked across the green marble lobby. After a few weeks away, the place did look good to her eyes. And that odd settled comfort in her belly welcomed her home.

The elevator door opened as soon as she walked up to it, as it often had since she'd held that stone wand and recited the words written upon it. She paused for a second, tempted to head to the stairs and continue building her legs back up.

May as well get used to this, especially if the silly thing was going to give her special treatment.

As soon as she stepped inside, a woman's voice called out from behind her.

"Hold the elevator, please!"

She grasped the door and leaned out.

A lovely woman with rich brown skin and long curly hair walked as fast as she could with a suitcase and a backpack. Elenda immediately felt guilty about Dwight and his assistant dealing with her travel bags. She pushed the door open button and grabbed the suitcase.

"Thank you so much," the woman said, panting. Under her coppery winter coat, she wore an ankle length burgundy skirt and a paler shirt that somehow made the flush in her cheeks even more appealing. "This thing can take a while if you miss it."

"No worries at all. What floor?"

"Seven."

As the door closed, Elenda caught her perfectly normal reflection in the glass. Her tanned face, her own cheeks flushed from the sudden cold, her bright and happy eyes. Warmth flooded through her as she recognized the scenario. A perfect recreation of the vision she'd seen in the elevator the first day she'd visited the vault with her grandmother.

For a second, fast enough that she wondered if she imagined it, she saw her multi-great grandfather instead of the floors moving past. He stared right into her eyes. His serious, stony expression transformed into a warm smile, every bit as lovely as her father's.

Elenda never would have suspected Liam had it in him. Her smile mirrored his as she turned to her right. "My name's Elenda."

## ABOUT KARI

Kari Kilgore's wanderlust and imagination lead her all over the world on grand adventures. Her heart and family bring her home to her native Appalachian Mountains of Virginia. From that solid base, she and her husband Jason A. Adams bring those adventures to life in fiction.

Kari writes fantasy, science fiction, and horror, and she's happiest when she surprises herself. She lives at the end of a long dirt road in the middle of the woods with Jason, various house critters, and wildlife they're better off not knowing more about.

### The Confidential Adventure Club

For Kari's exclusive free After The End stories and deleted scenes, discounts, early pre-sale releases, adorable pet photos, and a whole lot more not available anywhere else, visit The Confidential Adventure Club at www.smarturl.it/c-a-club.

Hope to see you there!

www.karikilgore.com
www.spiralpublishing.net

## ALSO BY KARI KILGORE

I hope you enjoyed reading *Legacy of the Land* as much as I enjoyed writing it. Check out more of my fiction at www.karikilgore.com.

### The Confidential Adventure Club

Want more fiction from Kari, including stories, discounts, and box sets not available anywhere else? Want to hear about locations, research, and other cool things that inspired this story and beyond? All that and adorable pet photos, too?

Join The Confidential Adventure Club and get a thank you gift of a free short story and a whole lot more at www.smarturl.it/c-a-club.

Hope to see you there!

### Novels:

*Until Death*

*The Dream Thief*

*Dreaming the Storm: Book One of the Storms of Future Past Series*

*Joining the Storm: Book Two of the Storms of Future Past Series*

*Fighting the Storm: Book Four of the Storms of Future Past Series*

### Novellas:

*Songs in the Mountain*

*Restricted Species*

*The Becalmed*

*In the Pines*

*Into the Storm: Book Three of the Storms of Future Past Series*

### Short Stories:

*Renovations*

*Intentions*

*The Garbage Belt*

*The Seeds of Love*

*Wicked Bone*

*The Sound of Murder*

*Terminalia*

*Little Five: A Terminalia Story*

*Reflections*

**Collections:**

*Fantastic Women: A Dark Fantasy Novella Trio*

*Fantastic Shorts: Volume 1 - A Fantasy Short Story Collection*

> "Kari Kilgore is an author to watch—her lyrical voice a siren song; her insight, conjured voodoo."
>
> —Richard Thomas, author of *Breaker* and *Tribulations*